Chilled to the Bone

An Ice Cream Truck Mystery
Book 1

Virginia K. Bennett

To the members of the writing community who supported
me early on, thank you!

Skye Jones
Marissa Farrar
Dawn Edwards
Kat Reads Romance
Kathryn LeBlanc
TL Swan
VR Tennent
Gina Sturino
Rachelle Kampen
...and so many more!

Table of Contents

Chapter 1

The Origin

"Sign here." The used-car salesman slid a stack of paperwork across his desk and pointed a pen at the line where Katie needed to provide her autograph.

"With pleasure."

Katherine Eileen Thorne signed her full name in exchange for an ice cream truck. And not just any ice cream truck—one with a loft bed in it.

"Here are your keys, and the truck is yours."

Katie thanked the man who had just made her recently discovered dream come true.

As a woman in her mid-forties who had never settled down, never purchased a home, never signed up for the American dream, she drove by a dealership for used cars one day and discovered a pink ice cream truck. What she saw in that ice cream truck was a new future. She turned her car around, pulled into the lot and made a deal to trade in her car for an adventure.

With a full tank of gas and no experience, Katie

pulled out of the lot with her new acquisition. The truck was in pristine condition, apparently sold to the dealership when the previous owner needed to move in with her elderly grandmother. It was Katie's good luck that she happened to drive the way she did that morning. Learning to drive the ice cream truck when she had previously driven a Ford Focus was an adventure all in itself.

The apartment Katie had been renting on the coast of Maine for the past eleven months was about to become unavailable when the landlord announced she was raising the rent by two hundred dollars at the end of May. In the past, Katie would have simply looked around for another apartment and another part-time job to fill the void. This time, she bought an ice cream truck she could live in—partially, anyway.

"Jaspurr, where are you?" she called as she opened the door to the apartment with boxes scattered everywhere, some full and some empty. The orange ball of fur and energy popped his head out of a box in the adjacent dining room and turned to look at Katie. "Want to see where we're going to live next?"

Jaspurr hopped out of the box and ran over to a leash and harness hanging from a wooden knob next to the door Katie had just entered. He bumped it with his face first, then his bottom and tail, trying to knock it off the peg.

"Not today, huh, Jaspurr?"

In true orange-cat form, he looked up at her and made a noise that resembled a bark—definitely not a meow. Jaspurr didn't meow. There were a number of sounds that he did make, one even resembling the word food, but there was no meowing in his vocabulary. At a sleek seven pounds, Jaspurr was ready for anything. The highlight of his day spent in the apartment was threatening the birds that landed outside his windows. With a strange cackle, he would warn them of their impending doom, only to watch them fly away safely moments later.

Katie removed the harness, placing it on the floor. Jaspurr ducked his head and stepped into the harness like he had done hundreds of times before. Grasping the other end of the leash, Katie walked out of the apartment and over to her new ice cream truck for Jaspurr's perusal, her old license plate in hand.

When she got inside the back of the truck, she realized just how shiny and new everything was. There were long freezers on either side of the center aisle with extended windows that opened over both. Jaspurr hopped up on top of the freezers behind the driver's side and plopped his bottom down, wrapping his tail around his hind legs.

"Is that your side?" she asked, reaching up to pet him. He bumped his head into her outstretched hand, giving his blessing. Katie knew he approved because a small nip would have followed had he not—nothing to break the skin, just a communication nip. In this case, he followed the head bump with a strut along the closed lids then leapt to the other side. Katie opened the freezer lids from the side recently vacated and counted how many tubs of ice cream she expected to fit.

3

While Jaspurr explored, Katie took down the ladder allowing access to the loft bed. Having only looked at it from below when purchasing the truck, she figured it was a good idea to see just how it felt to lay up there. Once horizontal, she decided it was good enough—not too tight to make her claustrophobic but not as big as she would like for storage.

"Jaspurr, can you get up here?" She tapped her short fingernails along the platform that supported her mattress. From the top of the freezer on the passenger side, Jaspurr easily vaulted onto her chest. "I guess that's a yes." After checking out the four corners of the mattress and the small cubical shelving beyond the twin frame, he started making biscuits on the stomach area of her hoodie.

She sat up quickly, not wanting to imply she was staying as long as Jaspurr was willing to stay. "We need to start figuring out what we really need in the truck because space will be limited."

Katie had hopped from apartment to apartment as an adult, always making decisions for what to keep and what to donate or throw away. This change, however, would be massive.

Turning backward to descend the ladder, she made her way to the first level of the truck. Knowing Jaspurr could take care of himself, she folded the ladder up and stepped into the cab of the truck. She had always taken Jaspurr with her in the car, but this would be a much more permanent road trip requiring some thought about how he could be kept safe from himself—due to his orange-cat behaviors.

She had taken the car harness for Jaspurr out of the Ford Focus she left at the dealership, but it didn't really fit the front seat of the truck. Pulling out her phone, she searched online for a seat-belt system for her feline friend that would be appropriate for their new mode of transportation. Katie clicked the purchase button and returned to the stainless-steel portion of the vehicle. Noticing her old license plate on the freezer lid, she found a spot to display it, the letters reading JSPURR, above the window for selling ice cream.

"Jaspurr, come on down now. We need to start packing." She took another look at the plate, admiring the lobster and wondering if she'd be as happy with her new plate once the temporary ones ran out. It was fortunate that she still had the apartment for the rest of the month, allowing her to receive her new plates before heading out to live her new life.

Jaspurr, who had made himself comfortable on the fresh mattress, refused to look at Katie. He had snuggled up into a circle of orange fur and tucked his face under his tail. When Katie pulled the ladder to climb up and get him, he startled and jumped down on his own. She gathered him up, collected the leash and harness, and returned to the apartment.

"You'll have fewer windows to enjoy in the truck, but I'm sure you'll get used to it." What she meant was Jaspurr would have fewer window seats. He couldn't be trusted not to escape when she had the sales windows open, so he'd be either on his leash or in a restricted part of the truck during business hours. As an exchange, he'd get to go on so many new walks and adventures when she wasn't working. Owning an ice cream truck meant Katie could choose her hours and location without needing to check in with anyone.

"What will our first adventure be?" she asked when they were back inside and seated at the table for two in the kitchen, phone in hand.

Jaspurr ran over to a shelf of travel books near the door Katie had collected over the years. When someone told her about their own great adventures, she'd often grab several books about that destination and immerse herself in everything she'd need to know when she visited—someday. He used a paw to pull all the travel books onto the floor.

"Jaspurr, we can't drive the ice cream truck to Scotland or Spain. I think we should try somewhere local while we work out the kinks." She got up and replaced the books he had pulled out then returned to her seat.

And there would be a lot of kinks to work out. Katie needed to get the truck cleared for food service, learn all about taxes for a self-owned business and decide how much product to buy before her first day serving.

She grabbed a notepad and started writing down everything she could think of. Jaspurr had other plans and dragged a magazine over to her feet. "What's this?"

Katie picked up the free magazine she had collected at a rest area. She liked to read through the ads to find new places to eat. She had friends, mostly acquaintances, that she chatted with at her current job or in passing, but she often found herself dining alone. The idea of going out to dinner with people seemed attractive, until it came to agreeing on where to go. This way, Katie got to choose exactly what she wanted on any particular day at any time she pleased.

Flipping through the magazine, she came across an ad for a retirement home on the coast about thirty minutes north of her apartment.

"This is perfect, Jaspurr. I bet we could get in touch with the recreational therapist and show up for a scheduled trial run. We could sell it as a nostalgic event for the residents to come out and buy ice cream and enjoy the nice weather. It would also be close enough to home where we could bail out if things weren't working." Jaspurr jumped up on her lap and purred. "I'll take that as a yes."

She continued to write down all the logistics it would take to get the ice cream truck up to code for selling, but also what she absolutely couldn't live without if she were gone for a long period of time. The truck might have a bed, but it didn't have a shower or toilet. Her list was getting quite long when she decided to take a break and call the retirement home. If nothing else, she'd leave a message to get the ball rolling.

"Good afternoon, Pine Knoll. This is Randall Quagmire at the front desk. How can I be of assistance today?"

Katie decided from his voice alone that she was really going to like Randall. "Mr. Quagmire, I was wondering if I might speak with your recreational therapist. Do they have office hours, or should I leave a message?"

"Are they expecting your call? I'm sorry, what's your name, Miss..."

"Ms. Katie Thorne. Pretty sure I'm too old for Miss, but thanks for the confidence boost. They are not expecting my call."

Randall chuckled. "Let me see if I can find her. Miss Jenny Lynn can be a little bit of everywhere." He placed her on hold, subjecting her to a knock-off version of rock music from the seventies.

The phone crackled. "Ms. Thorne, I'll connect you to Jenny now."

"Thank you very much, Randall. I hope to be seeing you soon."

"Of course." The line went an odd silent, like Katie imagined a vacuum in space might sound—or a lack of all sound as the case may have had it.

"Good Afternoon," sang the female voice. "You've got Jenny on the line. How can I help you today?" She sounded as if she was once a radio DJ. Katie decided to reserve judgement until after she got through her self-promotion schtick.

"Miss Lynn, my name is Katie Thorne, and I recently purchased an ice cream truck. I was wondering if I might make arrangements with your retirement home to set up in your parking lot as a scheduled activity for a couple days. You know, bring people back to when they were kids and provide a social setting for guests to gather." She paused, allowing Jenny the chance to respond or at least think about the proposal for a moment. It took all of Katie's restraint to withhold from blathering on and on about how great of an idea it was.

"I think that sounds like a wonderful activity. Let me run it by the director. Now, before we get ahead of ourselves, what's the cost breakdown?"

"I'm just starting, and a huge part of this is for me to learn. I'm open to letting the guests pay, letting your budget supplement costs to get them down to something you deem more reasonable for your guests or letting you cover a maximum cost for however long it lasts. I hope this is an event we can both benefit from."

The conversation ended with the guarantee of a call back from Jenny and positive vibes. Since Katie couldn't guarantee a gig, she kept looking for other options to explore, and with Jaspurr now curled up on her lap, she was in-cat-pacitated, needing to wait out the latest nap after disturbing the one in the truck.

Things were looking positive for this new phase of Katie's life.

Chapter 2

The Agreement

OVER THE COURSE OF THE NEXT WEEK, KATIE efficiently packed up what she wanted to donate and sold a few items on social media, saving up for the first major purchase of materials her ice cream truck would need. The hardest things to eliminate were knick-knacks.

It seemed like everything Katie picked up had a memory or a story. One figurine had been passed down from her grandmother, but it wasn't anything she actually liked looking at. Another tricky decision was about a painting that her best friend from college had given to her as a birthday gift. It was a nice painting, and a nice gift at the time, but she didn't really see that person any longer nor did she have any attachment to the subject of the painting. Both ended up in a donation bin.

Once she had gone through most of the random tchotchkes, her wardrobe came next. Like most middle-aged women, Katie had a large selection of they'll-fit-again-someday clothes. Nothing in this pile would fit in the small cubbies of the ice cream truck loft. If it didn't currently fit, it went in a bag of donations. Somehow, that was easier than it had ever been before.

The truck had a twin mattress, so she'd need to get rid of all bedding, except her very favorite pink blanket. She knew it was a full-size comforter, but it was the one item she still had from college that she loved. Jaspurr loved it too. When it was cool enough for the pink blanket to come out, she knew it was going to be a nice long nap for him. Currently, the pink blanket spent most of its time in a closet because the weather had already warmed up, but it would hold a place of honor at the foot of her new bed three hundred sixty-five days a year—plus one on leap years.

She kept three bath towels, three hand towels and three washcloths, assuming she'd be able to do laundry often enough for that to work. If it didn't, she'd have to adjust. Since they would be stored in another cubby, she kept only the purple ones. Purple was her favorite color, and she'd have preferred a purple ice cream truck if there had been a choice, but pink would have to do. If all went well, maybe she'd be able to afford to paint it in the future.

Toiletries ended up being easy because Katie wasn't all that into primping and pruning. She didn't paint her nails, though she always kept them looking nice. Her blonde hair was off her shoulders, but not by much. She had spotted her first gray hairs recently and was totally fine with it, content with where she was in life. She didn't feel like anything was missing or lacking, so a few gray hairs weren't about to throw her into a tailspin. What she did wish for was the ability to throw the ten extra pounds she just couldn't shed into a donation bin.

If she were brutally honest with herself, eating good food was much more important to her than the ten extra pounds. She enjoyed cooking, and that was probably what she would miss most about having the truck in place of an apartment. The space would allow for a little storage in the stainless-steel section, so she'd need to look into an induction burner and maybe one pot and one pan. An instant pot might also be a good investment. Refrigeration certainly wouldn't be a problem, so cooking her favorite foods might still happen.

"Jaspurr," she said as she folded the remaining clothes she was keeping, "we'll have to go for more walks and spend less time in front of the television. Deal?" Jaspurr twitched an ear and nothing more. She didn't know if that was a positive or negative response, but she'd gladly cross that bridge—leash in hand—when she came to it. A tablet and an unlimited data plan would take the place of her television and cable bill.

The call back from Jenny at the Retirement home came mid-week, while Katie was weeding out all of the unnecessary items she'd carted around from apartment to apartment. She confirmed that Katie could park in the side parking lot, under a large maple tree, and they would set up a schedule for guests living at the retirement home to come out. They even offered to create a pop-up seating area around the truck to make it more enticing for the guests to check out Katie's offerings. With a silent fist pump, she graciously accepted and planned to show up the following Friday morning to give her time to get ready.

In exchange, Katie requested the use of an electrical hook-up as well as a place to get ready in the morning and evening. She knew, technically, she could drive home, but she wanted to make this trial run as realistic as possible. The reality Katie was facing involved a lot of unknown factors, and she wanted to test them out while she still had an apartment to fall back on. Jenny agreed she could utilize the locker rooms in the fitness center for the duration of her stay. Neither Katie nor Jenny had organized something like this before, so it was all new to both of them.

When the details had all been ironed out, Katie started contacting wholesale companies to order the products she would need. At least the product was ice cream, so as long as she could keep it frozen, it would carry over until her next gig. In addition to seeking out places to set up her mobile shop, she'd make her truck available to rent for parties and events. She decided weddings sounded fun and decided to look into advertising with wedding planners in New England.

Katie spent the next week getting those pesky forms filled out and inspections done along with all of the purchasing required to stock the truck. When it needed to be plugged in, she used an outlet at the apartment complex she lived at—not knowing who was paying the electric bill on that outlet. The final items she wanted to pack in the truck were neatly stowed away, and she had received the safety harness for Jaspurr in the mail. Because she didn't know how he would do when she opened the truck for business, she also purchased and installed a netting system to keep the loft-bed area as a restricted location when needed.

"I think we're all set, Jaspurr." Picking him up and giving him a snuggle, she took one last look at the nearly empty apartment. She still had furniture in each room, but that was about it. "Let's skip the harness since we're going right to the truck." She picked up the leash and harness but carried it along with Jaspurr to the truck. Once she opened the passenger-side door, she dropped the leash on the floor and figured out how to secure her passenger princess—or prince, as the case may be. He was able to stretch out just enough to put his front paws on the dash.

Katie walked around to the driver's side and clambered in, wishing she had a step to make the ascent easier. Like the dutiful forty-something she was, each mirror placement was assessed before even starting the vehicle. She checked on Jaspurr, still stretched out as far as his front legs would reach, and turned the key in the ignition. "Here we go."

The thirty-minute drive was smooth and uneventful. When she pulled into the parking lot of The Pine Knoll Retirement Community, she decided that retiring here someday was a new life goal. The four-story structure sat high above a beach and had the most spectacular view of the ocean. To one side was a street, but the other was a grassy area that went on for at least the length of a football field. She was able to quickly identify the maple tree she was allowed to park under.

Because she didn't know exactly where to set up her truck, she parked across several paved spaces, took Jaspurr for a quick walk and went in to find Jenny Lynn—after securing Jaspurr behind the mesh barrier with the air conditioning still running. Before she could get to Jenny, she first crossed paths with Randall Quagmire and a sign reminding all visitors to stop at the desk and speak to the attendant first.

"Good morning. How may I be of assistance?" His smile stretched from ear to ear revealing sparkling white teeth, including a small gap between the two front ones.

"Good morning to you too. My name is Katie..." Before she could finish her two-syllable name, Randall was speaking over her and rushing around the corner of the semi-circle desk.

"Katie Thorne, as I live and breathe. Everyone is looking forward to your visit. We've been promoting it all week." He gave her two air kisses before she even knew what was happening, grasped her right arm at the elbow and wrist and began to escort her down a hall, the quick pace of his speech pattern matching the pace of his steps.

"Good to know. I was wondering if we were..."

"Going to see Jenny? Of course. She has checked three times if I've seen or heard from you. She'll be just thrilled to know you've arrived. She had someone move the tables and chairs out for you already, but if they need to be adjusted, just let her know." He stopped, suddenly, in front of a closed door at the end of the hall, Jenny's name on a name plate beside it.

"I guess I'm all set, Randall. Thank you so..."

"Oh, you're very welcome."

Katie realized that full sentences didn't happen around Randall. She knocked on Jenny's door, not wanting to start another thought that would go unfinished.

"Come in."

"I'm all set, Randall. Have a nice day." She rushed the words to make sure she got all of them out.

"I'll see you outside soon. I can't wait to get an ice cream." He did a quick series of quiet claps in front of his face, turned and shuffled away.

Katie opened the door to a small but bright office. She knew from the way Randall turned, it wouldn't have an ocean view, but at least the window was large and had the ability to open—the smell of the salt water strong.

Jenny was sitting at her desk, pouring over financial spreadsheets, so absorbed in the work she didn't look up. The snick of the office door closing caught her attention enough to shake her out of her one-track focus. She visibly shook her head before checking over her shoulder.

"I'm sorry, you are?"

"Katie Thorne. You were expecting me with the ice cream truck today."

"I hadn't laid eyes on you yet; of course you're Katie Thorne." She stood and extended her arm, grasping Katies from where it hung at her side. Her handshake wasn't too firm, but it startled Katie. "We have everything

16

ready for you." When she let go of Katie, Jenny gestured to the door for them to leave, Katie needing to leave first due to a lack of space.

She took the hint, opened the door, and headed back in the direction of Randall's desk.

"Let's not do that. We can leave through the emergency exit. As long as the door closes in under ten seconds, the alarm won't sound." The thought of setting off a security alarm made Katie nervous.

Jenny pushed the door open and held it for Katie who practically jumped through, allowing Jenny to close it after about seven total seconds. The two women walked around the building, heading back to the maple tree and Katie's ice cream truck.

"I know Phil already got the tables and chairs set up, and he was planning to leave an electrical cord for you to plug your truck into. Did you need anything else? You can use the fitness center as soon as you want."

"Actually, one of the freezers seems to be not staying as cold as it should. Would it be possible to put a few of the tubs in your walk-in freezer until I can go through some of the product?"

"Not a problem. Let's grab the first couple, and I'll walk you there. After, we can get you the lay of the land so you know where you are. The first scheduled opening for you isn't until four, so you should have plenty of time to get settled."

"Perfect."

Katie and Jenny went to the back of the ice cream truck. When Katie opened it, she grabbed a tub of chocolate chip ice cream first then a tub of vanilla, one for each woman to carry.

"I'll come back after for the third," she said, grabbing the vanilla for herself.

Jenny walked to the front door, scanned a card then struggled to open it. Katie noticed the blue button with a picture of a wheelchair and pushed it, opening both sets of doors for them.

"Already making yourself at home," Jenny commented.

They walked past Randall, neither of them making eye contact. Along the next hallway, they passed the entrance to the fitness center on the left, which Jenny pointed out, and made their way to the back of the building where the kitchen was. Katie continued to carry her tub of ice cream, but Jenny needed to set hers down, the freezer door requiring a little more muscle than she could muster with her arms wrapped around the frozen treat.

Swinging the door open, Katie went to step right in while Jenny still needed to pick hers up.

A shriek burst from Katie's throat in a way she didn't know was possible, and the tub of vanilla ice cream almost crashed to the floor when she lost her balance for a moment. Lying on the concrete was a man, possibly older than Katie, a concerning shade of blue on his face.

Katie yelled, "Get the EMTs here, now!"

Chapter 3

The Ingredients

KATIE DIDN'T KNOW WHAT TO DO. BOTH SHE AND Jenny were holding huge tubs of ice cream—not really life or death—but she wanted them to stay frozen. She stepped around the body and placed her tub on the very back, bottom shelf.

"Jenny, hand that to me so you can go call 9-1-1." It was both the right thing for Jenny to do and the right thing for a business Katie hadn't even technically started yet.

"Right." She passed the tub over the body and ran as soon as it was released from her fingers. Katie, placing it next to the other tub where she thought it would stay coldest, looked down at the face of a stranger.

The man she now assumed to be dead was far too young to be a resident at the retirement community. He was lying in a way that suggested he had chosen the position, almost as if he had decided to take a nap on the floor of the walk-in freezer. The color of his skin had started to turn blue and frosty, suggesting he had been in there for a while. Why was Katie so drawn to the situation? Why didn't she just leave the freezer and wait for someone else to show up?

In the long line of jobs Katie had held, she included on her resume medical transcriptionist and secretary. Being a secretary wouldn't normally be something that led to an inquisitive streak when discovering a dead body, but it did if you had been the secretary for a funeral home. Neither job had lasted particularly long—none of Katie's jobs ever seemed to—but they had lasted long enough for her to pick up some general knowledge about death.

He had a light sweater on over what appeared to be a t-shirt based solely on the collar Katie could see, and the sleeves were wrapped over his hands like a small child would who had refused mittens before heading to school. The sweater was also tucked fully around his front, as much as it could be, held tightly against his torso by criss-crossed arms. Whoever he was, this didn't appear to be someone unsuccessfully trying cryotherapy for the first time. If Katie were to guess, he was an employee and this was his work outfit for the day, or maybe even last night.

The door to the freezer was still wide open, and she could tell it was already starting to warm up in the freezer. The time she'd have alone with the body had to be running out. Bending closer to the face, it looked like maybe this man had a black-and-blue eye, but that could have just been discoloring from the cold. He had short hair on top of his head, no balding spots apparent, and a well-kept beard. There just had to be a story behind this, and Katie hoped to be around long enough to learn what that story was.

A commotion could be heard in the distance. As it got closer, Katie decided she should be at the door when they showed up, not hovering over the deceased. Carefully, she tiptoed back to the front of the freezer just before the trio of EMTs turned the corner. She backed up, allowing them entrance. Jenny was right behind the third man and Katie joined her in the hall.

"I can't believe you were in there with him. I'm so sorry, and this being your first day here."

"Who is that man? Did you recognize him?"

"His name is Philip, well, *was* Philip. He is the night-time clerk at the front desk. Typically, he leaves at eight when Randall arrives. Randall never mentioned anything about Phil this morning."

Katie wondered if Philip was never seen by Randall so there wasn't anything to mention. When you worked together for a long time, people often covered for each other. Maybe Randall just thought Phil slipped out early and didn't want to get him in trouble. Another theory was that Randall did check out with Phil and something happened to him after. Katie decided she wanted to stay close to Jenny or Randall as much as possible. She thought about the state of her truck. If she needed to open the window at four and start serving immediately, she was ready. Jaspurr had been walked right before she entered, and had fresh water and food, so he'd be all set until at least four as well.

Behind Jenny was a police officer. When he approached the pair, Katie noticed the badge read Sullivan. He looked like an officer with some experience but maybe not a lot. He had no wedding ring, and Katie decided to put a pin in considering why she noticed that so quickly. A clean-cut look made her think military experience, but anyone could have a close fade.

"Ladies, I need to ask you a few questions."

"Anything at all," responded Jenny too quickly. "Leonard, this is Katie. She's the owner of the ice cream truck in the parking lot. She's just here for the weekend, but she's the one who first saw the body."

"Thank you for that. Do you know who it is she found in the freezer?"

Officer Leonard Sullivan, Katie had surmised, was holding a pad of paper and a pen he had begun to chew on. He didn't have any reason to be nervous, so it must have helped him think, she thought to herself.

Jenny hesitated a little and responded, "His name is Phil, Philip Rainey, if you need his full name. He works at the front desk during the graveyard shift and does general tasks around the property. Last night, he got the tables and chairs ready for Katie's arrival."

"Do you know when he was last seen?"

Jenny paused. "I think you'd have to ask Randall. I don't typically see Phil when I get in at nine, but I'm pretty sure Randall does. I know he worked last night because he was the one I asked to move the tables and chairs, but I didn't actually see him do it. I leave before his shift starts. I'm sorry I'm not more help, Leo."

Katie picked up on the name change. First, Katie had called him Leonard when she introduced them, but now she was calling him Leo. It might have absolutely nothing to do with her visit to The Pine Knoll Retirement Community, but she wasn't letting any details sneak by.

"Jenny, as long as you tell me everything you remember, that's the best I can ask for. Now, Katie, what do you remember?"

"I remember Jenny had to open the door even though we got there at the same time. She put down her ice cream because there was a handle she had to open, then picked it back up. It wasn't a lock, but it clearly kept the freezer door closed. If you test it out, Officer Sullivan, I'm pretty confident Phil wouldn't have been able to open it from the inside."

"That's a common misconception. These freezers have built-in safety features now to prevent that very thing from happening. I'll look into it, but I appreciate your attention to detail. What happened after the door was open?"

Katie was a bit ruffled by his challenge to her observation. It wasn't about who was wrong or right, she just didn't expect him to do anything but ask questions. Once she had a moment to collect herself, she continued.

"Well, I went in first, holding a large tub of ice cream, ten gallons to be exact."

"Sounds heavy." He dropped his pen and his eyes to the paper.

"They are. I carried one and Jenny carried the other. We were bringing them to the walk-in because one of my freezers in the truck was on the fritz. After I saw the body, I walked around it to place by tub in the back then took Jenny's so she could call 9-1-1."

"Why not have her set it down and call? Why go to the back of the freezer where you'd need to step over the body?" He was now locking eyes with her, determinedly searching to see if she was telling the truth when she answered.

"I was trying to think about everything at the same time. I needed my ice cream in the freezer, and this man might still have been alive for all we knew. We just couldn't tell from outside the door. By putting the ice cream in the back, the ice cream was more likely to get and stay frozen, and I would be able to check on him better. When I looked at Jenny, she was in shock. She could have put her tub down at any time, but I felt she wasn't going to. When I asked her to hand it to me, I got her attention and told her to go make the call."

"Did she leave right away?" He looked at Jenny then back to Katie.

"Yes, and I put the second tub of ice cream on the shelf, if you were curious. While she was gone, I looked at who I now know is Phil, and tried to take in all the details I could."

"What details were those?" Officer Sullivan became distracted at that moment by the EMTs. They had originally brought with them a long board and were currently trying to get the body onto it. "No. Don't move him. Is he already deceased? Can you help anything by moving him?"

"Sorry, Leo, he's way past helping."

Unfortunately, they had already started moving the body. Katie could easily see he was no longer in the same position she had found him.

"Don't touch anything else. Let's get forensics in here, and we'll need to get official statements from the two of you."

"More official than what you've been doing?" Jenny asked. Katie was surprised to hear her ask a question.

"Yes, Jenny, more official." Officer Sullivan scratched at his temple. "Jenny, do you have two offices we could use once I get a couple more officers on the scene?"

"Of course."

Jenny led them to the front of the building via a different hallway than she did on the way to the freezer, presumably to keep them out of the front lobby. Katie wanted in the worst way to ask Randall some questions, but there was no way she was getting out of Leo's line of sight to do that. It wasn't her job to investigate, but getting back to her truck before four was still imperative.

"Officer Sullivan, can you please interview me first? I'll tell you all the details I noticed and answer every question, but I really need to be at my truck before four to open on time."

The officer responded, "You should have plenty of time. It's only just past two now, and I'd be happy to conduct your interview as soon as we get someone else here to help."

"Thank you." She sighed.

Did Katie *need* to start at four? Not really. If Katie

had to cancel, it wouldn't be the end of the world, but she really did want to talk to Randall before she started working at the truck. Because she didn't want to ask too many questions, especially in front of Officer Sullivan, Katie started to think about the front-desk position.

If Randall typically came on at eight when he relieved Phil, Phil's shift must have started at midnight. There was one other front-desk person unaccounted for, at least during the week. It was likely that they had a completely different person or persons working Saturday and Sunday, but today was Friday. Katie made a mental note to find out who would have left at midnight when Phil arrived for the start of his shift.

"Leo, if you want to use my office for Katie instead of me, I totally understand. There is a second office on the other side of the hall, just here, and I can stay there. It's empty."

"That would be perfect. I assume Katie has no access to your computer or files if she's in there."

"That is correct."

Katie reassured him by stating, "I do have my phone, and I'm happy to hand that over if it's a problem."

"Shouldn't be." Officer Sullivan waved at another officer walking in their direction. "Frankie, down here." When she got closer, Katie noticed that Frankie was a woman—not that it mattered. "Officer June, Can you interview Ms. Lynn here about what she observed heading to the walk-in freezer and what she saw when she arrived?"

"I can do that."

Katie's quick read on Frankie was that she was all business. She also felt that Officer Sullivan might not want to interview Jenny, but she couldn't quite put a finger on why. Either way, she was going to do her best to efficiently answer whatever questions Officer Sullivan had for her so she could move along to something or someone more interesting—Randall Quagmire.

Chapter 4

The Unaccounted

KATIE MADE HER WAY DOWN THE HALLWAY, fingering the card Officer Sullivan had given her, and back to the lobby where Randall was still seated at the front desk. As he hadn't looked up yet, he also hadn't started talking. Katie knew she'd need to stand her ground so as to not continue getting talked over.

"Randall, did Phil check out with you this morning when you took over?"

He looked up from where he had been folding papers and sealing envelopes. "How do you know Phil?"

"I don't, but I do know he's on before you. Jenny was telling me about the place and how everything runs. Just catching me up on some details before everyone comes out to the..."

"Oh, don't you worry. The residents will catch you up on all the gossip. You'll be fresh meat." He chuckled then openly laughed at his joke as if he was the first person to ever tell it and just discovered it was funny.

"So, what about Phil? See him this morning?"

"Does this have anything to do with the police and paramedics? Is everything okay?"

Katie leaned over the elevated counter. "If you answer my question, I'll tell you what I know."

By no means was Katie a busybody. She'd never found herself in a situation like this before and was shocked at her own behavior. There was no flirting—in that way—but she was certainly trying to exchange information in a way that would benefit her need to figure out what had happened.

Clearly agreeing to the terms, Randall leaned over, quite close to Katie, and spilled the beans.

"Phil has narcolepsy. He takes medication for it, but he is found sleeping on the job often. I'm sure it doesn't help that he works the graveyard shift, but there is an extremely attractive shift differential and very few interactions with the residents—an introvert's dream. What I hear is that he is one more infraction from getting fired. What do you know?" Randall was practically salivating to learn more dirt about Phil.

"I'm going to guess that Phil took his final nap on the job last night?"

"Did you overhear him getting reprimanded by Jenny again? Did he get fired?"

Katie inhaled deeply and exhaled over several seconds. "He died."

Randall guffawed at the two-word sentence. When he stopped long enough to look at Katie's very serious face, he held his hand to his chest. "You're joking, right?"

"Unfortunately, I'm not. I was bringing ice cream in with Jenny to store in the walk-in, and we found him lying on the floor of the freezer."

"Are the paramedics treating him?" Randall's eyes searched Katie's, looking for something other than the truth.

"He was already deceased when I found him."

"I knew Zeke said he'd kill for Phil's job, but I didn't think he meant it literally." Randall slid back into his chair looking lost.

Now it was Katie reading Randall's eyes, searching for the truth. "Who's Zeke?"

"Guess Jenny didn't get that far. Zeke's the guy who takes over when I leave at four. Randall held up his wrist, checking his watch. Should be here soon because he usually arrives early. We usually chat for a bit where I tell him anything that happened during the day that he might need to know. You know, residents who might try to pull one over on us because of the shift change."

"Sounds like working with children."

"Exactly. I'm mom and he's dad, but we've got them all figured out. Should be here any..." The door behind Katie opened, and possibly the most attractive man she had ever seen in person entered.

At over six feet tall, Zeke walked in with a relaxed swagger reserved for models and movie stars. The wrinkles around his eyes gave away his age, but somehow made him more handsome. His hair was long enough to cover his ears and the perfect shade of sandy blonde only surfers could pull off. When he ran his fingers through it, the waves on either side of his center part fell as if they were styled by Vidal Sassoon.

Katie silently reminded herself to pick her chin up off the counter and closed her mouth.

"Hey, Randall. What's with the police cars and ambulance in the parking lot? Seems a bit much. Did Mr. and Mrs. Rochester get in a fight again?" Zeke was joking around like he probably always did with Randall, but today wasn't just another Friday. "And what's with the ice cream truck? There is an orange cat sunning itself on the dash."

Before Randall could start, Katie busted into Zeke's musings. "I'm the ice cream truck. I mean, I'm the reason for the ice cream truck. Name's Katie Thorne. There's an event starting at four for the residents to come out to get ice cream from me. Jenny and I set it up as a trip down memory lane, we're hoping."

He reached out to shake her hand and held it a little longer than necessary, making Katie worry her hand would start to sweat if he didn't release it soon.

"Nice to meet you, Katie Thorne. Now that I think about it, I do remember something in the newsletter about ice cream. Do you have the frozen lemonade cups with the wooden spoon or the bomb pop?"

She could feel her cheeks heat and hoped they weren't too pink. "I scoop ice cream, so bowls and cones. Hopefully you'll come out later."

"You bet, if you've got anything vegan."

31

Katie began to panic. She hadn't even thought about vegan options, all she'd been worried about were allergies. "I'm not sure. Are there certain ones that are typically vegan?" She knew she couldn't say ice cream because cream pretty much implied it wasn't vegan, so she just tried to keep her response vague.

"Any sorbets? Those are mostly just fruit."

"Yes!" she said with far too much excitement. "I have a raspberry sorbet. Hope you like that flavor."

"Who doesn't?"

"Right. Umm, you also asked about the ambulance and police cars." She wanted to see if there was any dirt on this relationship, so she wanted to turn the discussion back around to something more important than ice cream.

He turned to ask Randall again, but Randal jumped at the chance to respond, both physically and metaphorically. He leapt out of his chair and raced around the corner of the counter to stand in a triangle with Katie and Zeke.

"Looks like Phil took his final nap on the job." He gave a long, exaggerated pair of winks to Zeke.

He whispered in response, "They finally fired Phil? Did they post the job? I've wanted to move to that shift since I started here."

What Zeke said sounded innocent—what Katie heard was motive.

"No." Randall sounded frustrated, but why would anyone jump straight to dead versus fired with Phil's employment history. "He's dead. Katie here found him frozen on the floor of the walk-in. Can you believe it?"

"Now I sound like a complete jerk. You've got to believe me, Katie, I wouldn't want anything to happen to Phil. I just wanted the graveyard shift because it's easier and pays better. Please, don't think less of me." His brown puppy dog eyes pleaded to her soul.

"I don't think anything about you. I just met you, and you don't give off the impression of a murderer."

"Who said anything about murder?" the two men said as if they had been practicing for the role of twins in a play.

"I didn't have time to tell you, Randall, but I don't think anyone would go into a freezer to take a nap. If the door closed behind him, he should have been able to let himself out. Officer Sullivan assured me those walk-in freezers have a system to prevent people from getting locked inside them."

"And did Officer Sullivan tell you that ours has been broken for months? We can't afford to fix it, so we've been using a brick to prevent the door from closing when we need to go in."

Katie didn't remember seeing a brick, and she was sure there was no reasonable way to get back there again until she sold an entire tub of ice cream. She'd need to keep asking questions to see if there was more to this than a man who couldn't help falling asleep.

"Maybe he was just so tired he forgot the brick," suggested Zeke.

"Why would he be in the walk-in at that hour

anyway? There is no reason to go in there for anyone at the desk, really. Maybe the kitchen staff would know."

Katie just saw roadblock after roadblock being put up. Not only could she not get back there to look for this incredibly important brick, but she also had no reason to go talk to the kitchen staff.

"I hate to gossip and run, but I need to go get ready for the residents wanting to take a trip down memory lane. Randall, I'm assuming I'll see you since your shift is ending. Zeke, will you be stopping by for some raspberry sorbet?"

"You've got it, as long as Randall hangs around long enough to cover for me." Both heads turned to check with Randall.

"I've got nothing better to do," he confessed.

"See you then." Katie turned, let herself out the front doors, and trotted out to the truck, checking first on Jaspurr who never should have made it to the dash.

She entered through the door at the back. "Jaspurr, where are you?" she cooed, not wanting to give away how much trouble he was in. Looking up to the mesh liner she had erected to enclose the bed, she noticed that a corner had been pulled away, allowing Jaspurr to freely explore the truck.

Once she had closed the rear door, Jaspurr could be seen stretching on his way toward the back area. He pranced over to Katie and rubbed his whiskers and tail across her legs, the whole time catching glances up to her face.

"You know exactly what you did. I'll be fixing that

before I open the window to serve customers." At that declaration, Jaspurr hopped up onto a freezer and rolled over, showing his beautiful white belly.

Most cats didn't like to have their bellies rubbed, or at least were semi-protective of their bellies, but not Jaspurr. If at all possible, he accepted any form of physical love. He was the best shoulder cat and would even lounge around the back of your neck if allowed. Rocking like a baby was also acceptable, as long as you rubbed his belly at the same time. Anyone looking for a cat to snuggle was welcome in Jaspurr's book.

As Katie was rubbing his belly, she noticed that the Velcro had been pulled apart and could have been open due to an operator error exploited by an intelligent feline. "I'll be watching you during this first shift. If you try to escape, you'll be stuck in the front seat belt until closing." She located his harness and leash to go for a brisk stroll before focusing on her first official opening.

On their walk, Katie tried to take in the surroundings. There were two tennis courts and what she assumed was a pickleball court, though she had never played either. The shuffleboard courts were adjacent to the parking lot, as were two pairs of horseshoe pits. The walkway down to the beach was long, but there were no stairs, so it appeared to be wheelchair accessible. She noted there was no pool, but she was pretty sure someone said there was an indoor pool—that made sense since they were in Maine. The property seemed extensive since the building had such a small footprint in comparison. She hadn't crossed paths today with a single resident yet. She figured afternoons might be a slow time for the retirement community.

A one-mile loop later, Jaspurr had done his business and Katie was ready to fix the escaping cat issue and serve up some ice cream. Now, if only she could get the scoop on Phil.

Chapter 5

The Options

As she dropped the window cover down to create a counter and pushed up the white and pink striped awning to give her some shade, Katie took a deep breath and appreciated all she had in this life.

Over her many years, she'd had every sort of part-time job and temp gig possible. The best job she'd ever had was working in an animal shelter. It was a paid position, but barely. The cats and dogs who were dropped off had some of the saddest stories, and her job was to turn their lives around. She found homes for dozens of dogs—some elderly and some just puppies—and probably hundreds of cats before the funding was slashed, causing the shelter to reduce their staff. She'd had a great apartment over the shelter so she could visit the animals at night whenever she wanted to, and that was a sad one to leave.

The worst job she could remember wasn't even all that bad. She had picked up a job as a custodian in a school once. The school was for grades pre-K through fourth, and the messes ranged from glue in the carpet to paint on the walls and some others much less pleasant. The amazing kids, however, made it all worth it. She loved how they'd give her high fives in the hall on the way to and from their specials, and how she even managed to end up in the yearbook—not a fancy high school yearbook, just photocopied pages stapled together. The yearbook was among the many items that didn't make the cut when she was weeding out unnecessary things that wouldn't fit in the ice cream truck.

She went to the back of the truck and snuck a peek at Jaspurr. "Just checking to make sure you haven't escaped yet." He was sleeping on top of a pile of towels stuffed into one of the cubbies. She wasn't even sure how he fit, but he was exactly where he was allowed to be.

The two-sided chalk board she bought for advertising purposes slid out easily. She hoisted it around to the front of the open window along with a box of chalk and plopped her bottom down on the grass to write out the flavors. In corresponding chalk colors, she wrote the names: Blueberry Buckle, Sweet Strawberries and Cream, Luscious Licorice, Sugar on Snow, The Almond Brothers, Banana Blitz, Death by Chocolate Chip, Vivid Vanilla and Raspberry Sorbet. She even added the logo so people—Zeke—would know it was vegan. Not wanting to go overboard on her first job, she stuck to flavors she thought would be popular for the audience. The third tub of ice cream from the malfunctioning freezer was forced to fit into another freezer, preventing Katie from making a return trip to the walk-in.

Before the clock struck four, and with Katie still writing flavors on the back side of the sandwich board, Randall sauntered up to check out the offerings.

"What do we have here?"

"Flavors are listed on the board, and I have plain cones, sugar cones, waffle cones and dishes."

"Sounds pretty straight forward. Didn't want to go mixing things up with something new and flashy?" He made jazz hands but kept his eyes on the chalkboard.

"Jenny and I wanted this to feel nostalgic, so I didn't want to go too wild. Did you want to order?" Katie climbed to her feet and brushed grass and dirt off her knees and back side.

"I'd like to, very much."

She walked around to the back and met him at the window, leaning on the counter to take his order. "And after I get your order, maybe you can tell me what you've been talking to Zeke about since I left."

"You drive a hard bargain, but I guess I can share. I'll have a single scoop of Banana Blitz in a sugar cone, please."

"Banana Blitz has ribbons of chocolate fudge in it. Is that..."

"Even better."

She washed her hands then opened her freezer for the first time—catching the attention of Jaspurr who let out a small bark—scooping a large sphere of ice cream that appeared to be slightly yellow with black tracks throughout. "That'll be four dollars, Mr. Quagmire."

He fished his wallet out of his back pocket and pulled out a five. "Keep the change for your tip jar."

"Awww, thanks." She hadn't even put out her tip jar yet, wondering if that would be seen as rude or greedy, but now that she had a single bill to put in it, she didn't feel as guilty. Handing over the cone wrapped in paper, she said, "Now, what's the scoop?"

The counter was almost too high for Randall to lean his elbow on, but he tried awkwardly then gave up. "I asked Zeke about last night. He did see Phil when he was getting ready to leave. Said everything seemed the same as any other night."

"So, we know he came to work on time. Did Zeke say anything about if he was sleepy when he saw him?"

"Didn't mention it, but Phil always seemed sleepy to me."

"Jenny told me she had asked Phil to get my tables and chairs set up, and they were ready for me when I got here, so he must have done that."

"I don't know. She sent that email to a group list, so technically anyone on the list could have done it. I'd suspect that's the case too, because Phil's not very reliable."

"Drat. I was hoping we had a little more to work with than we do. Anyone else who might have crossed his path after midnight?"

"I'll be gone, but when the residents start coming out, look for a short couple,"—he held his hand flat and horizontal below shoulder height—"wearing the loudest outfits you've ever seen."

"How can an outfit be loud?" Katie inquired.

"Trust me, you'll know. They are the Mitchells, and they tend to be up late taking walks and chatting. Drives the other residents nuts, but they're not breaking any rules.

"What would I be asking them, exactly?"

Randall sighed. "You wanted to know if anyone else had seen Phil. They'd be your number one suspects because of the hours they keep."

"If you're not here at night, how do you know?"

"We have security cameras in the residential areas. When something gets stolen or damaged, we watch the footage to see if we can figure out what happened."

Katie stared at Randall. "And you didn't think to watch the footage of last night and this morning yet?"

Randall, holding his ice cream cone in one hand, smacked himself on the forehead with the free hand. "No, and Zeke is in there, so it'd be weird if I went in."

"What if you offered to relieve Zeke so he could come get a cone. A kind gesture. I'll keep him occupied out here, and you check to see if there's any sign of Phil on the footage."

Randall started to walk back to the front doors then turned to face Katie again, back and forth at least three times before he said, "What if I'm not supposed to watch it? What if the police come asking for the footage?"

"Make something up. Say something was damaged and you're trying to figure out what happened." Katie

41

had started to talk with her hands, a sure sign she was getting worked up. "The longer you're out here with me, the more time the police have to collect the footage or Zeke has to destroy it."

Randall stopped dead in his tracks. "Why would Zeke destroy it?"

"How well do you know Zeke?"

Randall licked his Banana ice cream. A look passed across his face, dismissive first then quizzical. "He does want the graveyard shift, doesn't he? Said so himself."

Katie pointed at Randall. "Go send him to me, and I'll do my best to keep him busy so you can check the footage. If you don't find anything, offer it up to the police anyway, but see what you can find first."

"I'm on it." He walked away, this time with purpose.

Less than five minutes later, Zeke poked his head into the window. Taller than Randall, he had no problem resting his elbow on the counter. "Randall sent me out to get a treat. Nice guy, huh?"

"Very nice of him to think about you like that. What did you want to order?" Katie pointed to the list of flavors. "I have cones or a dish."

"Vegan, remember. Cones aren't vegan, so I'll have a dish."

Katie apologized. "I totally forgot. Sorry."

"Not a problem. I'd like a two-scoop raspberry sorbet, please."

"Coming right up." She opened a freezer lid. "While I have you here, what's the story with Phil? I heard he was near to getting fired before, well, you know."

Zeke went from a single elbow to both arms criss-crossed on the counter. "Yeah. He'd fallen asleep, not done his chores and all kinds of infractions, most of which were overlooked. I'm just glad I worked the shift before him."

"Why's that? Do you mean specifically last night?"

"Nah. I did my job and got my work done. Anything Phil failed to do fell on Randall. He had quite a lot to say about Phil each day when I'd show up for my shift."

"Interesting. Enough where he'd want to find a way to get rid of Phil?"

Zeke totally missed her implication or was a great actor. His focus was completely on Katie scooping his sorbet. "We both joked about Phil leaving so I could take the shift and make Randall's life easier in the process."

"So, you and Randall talked about getting rid of Phil?"

"Not so much. We talked about how much better things would be when they finally fired Phil." When Zeke caught Katie's eyes as she handed him the dish, he said, "What are you trying to suggest?"

"I'm suggesting you owe me six dollars for the two scoops. The chocolate chip really is to die for, but the raspberry sorbet is a great second choice since you can't eat it." She winked, breaking the tension.

"Of course. Now, I'm the one who forgot." He took out his wallet and found a five and a single in the pocket. "I should be getting back in there. Randall's at the desk for me, and he'll want to get going before everyone else starts to come out. The Mitchells are a piece of work. Did he tell you about them?"

"Funny you should mention the Mitchells. What's so notable?" Katie was curious because Randall's mention of their late-night adventures and loud clothes didn't seem like the same thing Zeke could possibly be referring to.

"No one else has a personality the size of Rita Mitchell, except maybe her husband, Karl Mitchell. They're quite the pair. You'll want to make sure you don't engage in a conversation with them. It may never end. You'll be a captive audience and fresh meat at the same time. Good luck."

"Thanks. Feel free to come out and save me if you see them."

"I might. Thanks for the scoops," he shouted over his shoulder as he walked away.

Realizing the types of cones should be listed somewhere, she went back outside to finish the chalkboard and add cone types as well, lifting up to her toes to make sure Jaspurr was still in his cubby.

While she was writing, Randall approached, but she could see residents starting to gather outside the front doors as well, potentially waiting for Jenny to give them permission to go to the truck.

"Before you get swarmed, I saw that just past midnight, Phil headed down the hall that leads to the walk-in freezer, but no one else was on camera. I did see when Zeke went off camera, but he could have gone down an employee-only hall that takes a longer route but still could lead to the freezer as well."

"Or he could have left work for the night," added Katie. "Any outside cameras?"

"I didn't check them. Geeze. I'm not working tomorrow 'cause it's Saturday, but maybe I'll stop in to relieve the weekend shift to come get ice cream and check the footage. What are your hours tomorrow?"

"I have my first availability at eleven. Does someone work then you could swap with?"

"I'll have to check the schedule, but expect me here before eleven tomorrow. I know it's not for a good reason, but this is kinda fun, right? As long as you don't tell anyone we're working on this, I won't let the cat out of the bag."

"We're in this together." They shook hands as the mob of retired residents made their way over to Katie's truck, ready to relive their childhood.

Randall quipped, "I'm gonna make like a banana and split."

Chapter 6

The Pair

THE RETIRED POPULATION AT THE PINE KNOLL Retirement Community covered quite the spectrum. Some residents looked too young to be there, moving as if their knees and back hurt way less than Katie's joints did. She was aware that she was way too young to feel so old, but also way too old to be acting this young, starting off on a new path like owning a traveling ice cream truck. Other residents were exactly what Katie had expected.

Walkers and scooters were apparent but not as many as Katie predicted. She realized, by observing the customers who came to her truck, that she had assumed this would be more like assisted living, and that assumption was incorrect.

"I'll have a waffle cone, dear. Could I please get one scoop of Death by Chocolate Chip and one scoop of Almond Brothers. You know, I was at their very first official concert. The Allman brothers, that is. I was with several other groupies and..."

"Margo, let the girl scoop your ice cream and get on with it." A woman with a head of tight curls nudged Margo's leg with her cane. "She'll talk to you all day if you let her."

"Ethel, why would you say something like that about me?"

"You mean the truth? She's running a business, and moving customers along is part of making money." She turned to address Katie. "You go ahead and ignore this one. We're all here for the ice cream, not the conversation."

Katie smiled politely. "While I scoop here, what can I get for you, Ethel?"

Ethel nodded. "Since I'm hoping to come the next two days, I'll only get a single scoop in a dish. Can't go overdoing it on the first day." She tipped her head to the side when Katie looked up, implying that Margo had been the one to go overboard with her two scoops in a waffle cone.

"Well, if you got out more and did some of the physical activities they offer, you could afford to have two scoops."

Katie stifled a laugh and handed the waffle cone over to Margo. "That'll be three dollars."

Katie had made a deal with Jenny when she offered to visit for the weekend. Jenny would use funds for their recreational program to offset the cost of the ice cream the residents ordered. The waffle cone Margo ordered should have been double the cost, but Katie dutifully kept track of exactly what was ordered to be able to get money back from Jenny on Sunday.

"Margo paid with exact cash, Katie wrote it down and Ethel repeated her order. "Single scoop in a dish, please."

"What flavor?" Katie leaned over and pointed at the list on the chalkboard.

"I'd forget my head if it wasn't still screwed on." She turned quickly and pointed at Ethel. "Not a single comment from the peanut gallery, you hear?"

"I would never... mention how you act so much older than I do even though you're, what, six years younger? Shame."

"So help me, it's a good thing you are the only one in here who can style my hair properly, or I'd spill all your secrets." Ethel turned back to Katie and placed a single dollar bill on the counter—the adjusted price for a single scoop. "Thank you, dear."

"I haven't scooped anything. You didn't tell me what flavor." Ethel started to look embarrassed this time. "I'll read you the flavors, and you can choose the one that sounds good." Katie read them, and Ethel stopped her on the raspberry one.

"You know that one's not actually ice cream, right?" goaded Margo.

"I don't care. Raspberry sounds like the flavor I would like." She actually stuck her tongue out in Ethel's direction. Turning back to the truck, she said, "Thank you, Katie."

Once she had scooped it into a dish, she passed it over the counter. "My pleasure."

The two women made their way to a table with two chairs under the maple tree. Katie thought for a split second, before the next patron stepped up, that she'd want to ask Jenny why it's called Pine Knoll if she didn't see a pine tree anywhere. The maple currently shading the area was beautiful, but not a pine tree.

Several cones and dishes later, Katie noticed a pair coming out of the front doors—he on a scooter and she with a walker. The pair wore matching Hawaiian shirts with the boldest patterns of red, yellow, orange and green. Her bottoms were jean capris, but he wore full slacks of the same kelly green that ran through his shirt. Both she and he finished their outfits with neon neckerchiefs. The back of his scooter sported a flag that must have been topping out around eight feet with a black letter M against the red triangle. The walker was wrapped in small twinkle lights like it was December instead of May.

When the colorful pair—obviously the Mitchells—made it to the front of her line, there was no one behind them. It was an odd feeling, everyone else sitting or returning to their space inside the retirement home, since there had been quite the boisterous community vibe less than ten minutes ago.

"Rita, so nice to finally meet you," beamed Katie, wanting to get ahead of the curve.

Instead of the expected response—a suspicious inquiry into how and why Katie knew Rita's name—she puffed up like a peacock. "Dah-ling," she cooed. "It's lovely to be met. How is your little truck doing today? Making lots of money, I hope."

"Staying afloat, thanks to Jenny."

Rita scrunched up her nose. "Jenny's not even out here. What does she have to do with your success?"

Katie wished there was a line of customers behind Rita so she had an excuse to move this along, but maybe Rita had some dirt she needed to dig up—or keep buried.

"Jenny's the one I organized my visit with. She's the reason I'm here."

From below the counter, she heard, "Jenny's the nicest one working here. She always takes the time to stop what she's doing and chat. Can't say the same about the rest of them."

Mr. Mitchell seemed potentially likable where Rita seemed, at best, tolerable.

"I'm going to assume this is Karl. Am I right?" Katie pretended to be on the fence, shimmying side to side like she might not be correct in her guess, her eyes squinted.

"You've got it, young lady. How did you hear about us?"

There it was. "You were one of the first people Jenny told me I'd want to meet." While this was wildly untrue, it would be a nice bump in Jenny's invisible capital and didn't take more away from Randall's, though his description was perfection.

"See." He elbowed his wife in the hip. "Told you that Jenny was a good egg."

"What can I get the two of you? Have you had a

chance to peruse the flavor and cone options?" Jenny leaned over the counter and pointed to the chalkboard.

Karl's scooter was blocking it, so he backed up. BEEP! BEEP! BEEP! The scooter was much louder than necessary for the circumstances, and exceptionally loud compared to other scooters Katie had already encountered today.

"I'll have Sugar on Snow. I'm assuming it's not really sugar on snow, but I'd be happy with either."

Rita spoke up. "Your dentures wouldn't allow you to have real sugar on snow anymore, Karl. That maple syrup turns to a substance harder to chew than the Salisbury steak on Friday nights. Katie, do you have real sugar on snow?"

"Regrettably, I do not. I'd love to have real sugar on snow, but I don't have an ice maker to simulate the snow. I'll keep it in mind for the future, though. This ice cream tastes like real maple syrup. It's delicious." She leaned over a little further. "Want to try a sample?" she whispered to Karl.

He leaned on the handlebars of his scooter. "I'd love to." He didn't quite wink, but it was close.

As loud as possible, Rita added, "And I'd like to try a sample of the Luscious Licorice. No one can get licorice-flavored things right, but I'll try." She looked around to the scattered residents sitting at tables. "Did you get licorice?" She pointed at a woman who reminded Katie of her own grandmother, frail but beautiful.

"I got Blueberry Buckle," the woman responded, sheepishly.

"I'll try a sample of that too," she demanded of Katie.

Making up the rule on the spot, Katie responded, "One sample only per customer. Which would you prefer?"

After a huff and a sharp look at Karl, she responded, "Licorice, I guess."

Katie wondered if she thought Karl might give up his sample, but she had quickly held it out over the counter before Rita was able to ask him outright.

"Karl, if you can't reach this, I'll gladly come around to bring it to you."

Rita was standing and had shown she was fully capable of letting go of her walker but made no move to take the sample and hand it to her husband. Karl struggled to stretch his arm out as far as he could, and they met in the middle.

"Thank you, young lady. Still got a little life left in this old body."

"Sure looks it." Trying to transition to the question she really wanted to ask, she said, "I heard that the two of you are often out later at night, walking and talking. Ever run into anyone? Not literally, Karl." She gave him the double-gun finger point, attempting to play to his good side.

"He's run into plenty of stationary items, but the people tend to jump out of the way. I'll take one scoop of licorice in a sugar cone. What will you have, Karl?"

"Two scoops of Sugar on Snow in a plain cone sounds delightful, Miss Katie. Thank you."

Katie had read them correctly. "Coming right up." As

she began to scoop, she asked, "Did you say that you did run into people on your late-night walks?"

Karl took a deep breath, appearing to prepare to answer, but Rita started first. "Mostly staff. Doesn't seem like we can get away from Zeke and Phil."

"Any chance you saw Zeke and Phil last night? Were you out and about?" She handed the sugar cone over to Rita with the single scoop of gray ice cream—possibly a little smaller than the single scoops previous customers had received.

"We were discussing the events of the day with Zeke at the desk when Phil came in, fifteen minutes late if you were curious." Rita took a taste of her ice cream. "Absolutely delicious. Well worth the risk, though I may get the blueberry tomorrow."

"Anything notable happen yesterday?" She swapped to a different freezer but kept a line of sight with the couple.

"Things about pool etiquette and door decorations, but nothing major for a Thursday. The good stuff usually happens on the weekends, but we only have the other desk attendants to talk to."

Katie walked out of the back doors of the truck to bring Karl's ice cream to him.

"Thank you. That's very kind of you."

"We don't have a line, so why not."

With a mouthful of Sugar on Snow, Karl said, "When Jenny stopped by, we chatted for a bit about you coming today."

Katie cocked her head to the side. "Jenny was there

when Phil showed up for his shift? After midnight? And Zeke was still there?"

"Yes. We usually only get to see Jenny when she's running about during the day, but she was much more relaxed last night. What did she say about the ice cream truck? Ahhh, an afternoon activity to help relive our youth. I can tell you, I'm appreciating this ice cream much more as an adult than I ever did as a kid." Karl took another bite and laughed at his own comment.

"I guess Zeke left pretty soon after Phil showed up, right?"

"We wouldn't know. Our visit was about over, so we moved on to the next part of our evening stroll," reported Rita, nursing her single scoop for all it was worth. "All three were at the desk when we left."

"Well, I do hope to see you tomorrow. It'll be three dollars for the two ice creams."

Rita was taken aback. "I thought Jenny said it was taken care of by the recreational committee."

"No, dear, she said they had taken care of some of the cost." Karl fished his wallet out of the front basket on the scooter. He grabbed a five and handed it to Katie.

"Keep the tip." This time she got a full wink and his pointer finger to the side of his nose, much like Santa Claus would.

"Why, thank you, dear sir. Enjoy your evening stroll—or roll—tonight, and I hope to see you both tomorrow."

The pair finished their ice creams about the same

time, even though Rita had a smaller amount and a head start. They turned to head back inside.

"Tomorrow it is," announced Karl.

As they made their way inside, Katie processed that Jenny was there last night before Phil died, and Randall must have lied about what he saw on the video. What was she going to do with this new information?

Chapter 7

The Denial

When the shift was done, Katie had scooped ice cream for around two hours and met many of the kind residents of The Pine Knoll Retirement Community. She enjoyed meeting people with all kinds of different personalities, hoping to run into some of them later that evening when she went in to use the facilities agreed upon with Jenny.

As soon as she closed up the window, she climbed the ladder to see Jaspurr.

"Hey, sweets. How was your evening?"

One at a time, Jaspurr stretched out his hind legs, then the pair of front legs at the same time. Once in the sitting position, he opened his mouth in a wide yawn. She had found him sleeping in a circle in the middle of the mattress. His sleepy eyes started to brighten up as she removed the mesh barrier restricting his movement about the truck.

"Want to go for another walk?" She was attempting

to make things better. He wasn't accustomed to being this restricted in his movements. Before the truck, he had a whole apartment to explore with many windows and soft spots.

Jaspurr slowly made his way to the edge of the mattress where Katie attempted to run her hand along his back. He flattened himself along the blanket, attempting to avoid her, and jumped down on top of the passenger-side freezer lid. His little strut along the stainless steel was topped off with a look over the shoulder when he reached the rear of the truck.

"You better get used to it. This is your reality as much as it is mine, at least for a while. I think you'll enjoy all the new places."

Just like he would at their apartment, he nudged the leash and harness that now had a spot near the rear door. This time, he managed to get it to fall to the floor and scurried into the harness on his own.

Katie nodded. "Good recovery. Let's go."

She opened the doors to a beautiful evening on the coast of Maine as soon as the harness was secure. Far below them, waves crashed into the rocky area that became a long, sandy beach. She couldn't remember Jaspurr ever getting to walk on a beach before, and they had noticed a path earlier that led down to the beach. After checking the signs, she'd ask Jaspurr if he wanted to touch the sand and ocean water, but not until she was sure it was allowed.

They walked almost a mile before the sign was visible

stating that pets were not allowed on the beach until after six in the evening and only when on a leash.

"Check and check," she said to Jaspurr, looking up at her from the sitting position he assumed when she stopped to read. If she didn't know better, she'd say he was giving her the stink eye, wondering what the heck she was checking. "The sign says you can go down onto the beach with me if you're on a leash. Want to feel the ocean?"

Jaspurr held the stare, as if trying to win a competition, then pulled on his harness to signify they were indeed walking down to the beach.

It was a lovely evening stroll, even if Jaspurr repeatedly picked up his paws to shake the sand from between his pads. When he touched ocean water for the first time, he leapt at least two feet into the air, trying to avoid landing back in the salty liquid, but it was too late. The wave was washing up as the first ripple caressed his sensitive forelimb so when he came down, all four paws landed firmly in the water. Jaspurr then climbed up Katie's pantleg.

"Oh no, you poor boy." She scooped him up before the nasty coldness could get him again. Refusing to be put down, Katie walked a while longer in the surf before ascending the path to return to her truck.

When they got back, she warmed Jaspurr with a towel before laying it on the passenger seat just in case he wanted a new view. She placed him on top of it gently, and he stared out the window in the opposite direction of where she sat in the driver's seat.

"You can't stay mad at me forever. I feed you." She got up and filled a bowl with food, placing it on the floor of the passenger side along with a full water dish. "You can wait until I've gone if it helps your ego." She turned, gathered her shower supplies and made her way to the front doors of the retirement home, noticing that the police vehicles and ambulance were gone. "Wonder when they left," she said to herself.

Entering the four-story building, she came face to face with Zeke.

"The sorbet was delicious. I'd keep that on the menu."

"Note taken. I bet you've been busy with residents going in and out the past couple hours."

"Busy, sure, but not difficult. What are your plans?" He pointed to the towel draped over her shoulder then the shower caddy of products in her left hand.

"Jenny said I could use the shower in the locker room while I was here. Did she not tell you?"

Zeke looked in the direction of Jenny's office at the far end of the hall. "She didn't. Did she give you a card for entrance?"

"No. I didn't know I'd need one. Is that a problem?"

Picking up the phone, Zeke said, "I'll just give her a call. I think she's still in her office."

Katie knew she was scooping until at least six and then went on a decent walk with Jaspurr. It seemed exceptionally late for Katie to still be at work on a Friday.

"Jenny, I've got Katie here, from the ice cream truck, and she said she had permission to use the locker room.

Uh huh. Okay, thanks." He hung up. "She said it's no problem. I'll go down there with you and let you in."

He started to stand when Katie said, "Will it be a problem if I need to come in during the night to use the restroom? Should I get a card?"

"There's always someone at the desk, so that shouldn't be a problem. I'll be here until midnight."

"With Phil, well, gone, who will take over at midnight?"

He sat back down, and Katie set her shower caddy down on the floor. "Since midnight becomes Saturday, the weekend staff come on. Sadie works midnight to noon Saturday and Sunday."

"Yuck. Two twelve-hour shifts. It's not enough to be a full-time job, and you lose your weekends."

"When you meet them tomorrow, it'll make sense. Also, they cover for people when they need a shift off or are sick, so they can still pick up extra time."

Katie thought about how Zeke wanted Phil's hours and it caused her to come up with new questions. "Either of them want a full-time shift? I mean, someone is already coming in at midnight, so the time wouldn't be a huge difference. Sounds like a great opportunity."

"Now I've got to worry about applying against people. Great. I figured they'd just let me switch."

Katie searched his eyes, trying to figure out if he was anxious or legitimately frustrated. From what she learned, Zeke wanted Phil's hours for the shift differential and so there would be fewer residents to deal with. The weekend workers might like the same, so if Zeke tried to get rid of Phil because of work, his plan might not have been as flawless as he hoped.

"Who is coming on at Midnight?" Hoping she didn't sound too nosey, Katie wanted to know who she might happen to run into should she need the bathroom later that evening or early the next morning.

"That's Sadie, who I mentioned. She'll be here at midnight. Only time I get to see her. She's really nice, but now I hope she's not looking for a switch to weeknights."

Katie shook her head to clear her thoughts. "Wait. You spoke to Jenny. She's still here?"

"Yes. Sometimes she stays late."

"Did she stay late last night too?"

Zeke looked up as if trying to recall. "Can't say I remember." Katie felt badly that Jenny felt very differently about Zeke than he felt about her.

"Didn't the police ask you any questions?"

"Why would they?" Zeke looked authentically confused.

"You worked the shift before Phil died, and you were the one to switch off when he got here. You viably could have been the last person to see him alive. How could they not have questioned you?"

"Well, I mean, I..." Zeke didn't have an answer for her though he was clearly searching. "I don't have a motive to kill Phil."

"Who said anything about killing anyone?"

"I thought that's what you were implying." They were both silent for a moment.

"I mean, I'm no detective, but didn't you say you wanted his shift?"

Zeke looked shocked with his mouth hanging open then angry with furrowed brows. "Wanting someone else's shift when I have a perfectly good job currently hardly seems like a reason to want to kill someone."

"There you go again."

"Didn't you come in here to use the locker room?" he asked, changing the subject.

"I did, but I'd love to talk to Jenny if she's available."

"If you want to go use the locker room, I'll see if she's planning to stay and if she's available."

"Just so I have an idea, has she stayed late recently?" Randall's information about Jenny being there last night was bouncing around in her mind.

"I don't keep track of her schedule."

Refusing to answer a question she knew he could easily answer, Katie checked that off as another piece of evidence worth noting. "Huh. Well, if you could point me in the direction of the locker room, that would be great."

Zeke stood and walked around the desk to let her down a hall that required a key card. Once they arrived at the door labeled 'Fitness Center,' he used his card a second time to get her in.

"There you go. I'll check on Jenny."

"Can you also see about getting me a card if she's still here?" I'd hate to bother Sadie more than necessary." She plastered a large, fake smile across her face, not breaking eye contact.

"I'll check on that too. Are you all set otherwise?"

"Yes, and thank you." She stepped into the fitness center leaving Zeke in the hall. The name was unfortunate because the room was small and consisted of only two treadmills, two stair climbers and a handful of free weights. She remembered back to when she was looking at this place online, and she thought there was a very different picture on the website. Either way, the locker room would have a sink, toilet and shower, all of which Katie desperately needed.

When she was finished getting ready for her first overnight in the truck, she thought about the hall Zeke had brought her down, and it was the same hallway Jenny had taken her down to get to the walk-in freezer. Knowing there were no cameras in the staff areas, she headed further down the hallway and turned a corner. However, Katie didn't recall Jenny using a key card again to get into the staff area that residents didn't have access to. When she got to that door, she realized she could go no further.

Turning around, she quickly noticed Jenny was checking the fitness center, probably for her. The glass door would quickly show her the room was empty, and turning her head to the side would expose Katie being in an area she didn't belong. As luck would have it, Jenny entered the fitness center causing Katie to bolt up the hallway, hoping to pass that door before Jenny came back out. If she got caught, she'd need to come up with an excuse quickly.

Katie burst through the door that emptied into the entryway adjacent to Zeke's desk.

"Did you see Jenny?" he asked. "She just went looking for you."

"She must have gotten distracted. Never saw her." Katie did her best to prevent Zeke from seeing her heart beating powerfully in her chest and hearing the quick pace of her breathing. None of that would make sense if she just finished showering and walked out to say good night.

"Weird. Well, why don't you wait here until she comes back. Shouldn't be too long."

"No problem."

They didn't pretend to be friendly like they were at their first introduction or at the ice cream truck, but they weren't talking about whether Zeke planned to take out Phil for his preferred time and pay. Katie would need to tread very carefully. Phil's death still could have been just a terrible accident, and she didn't want to start making enemies with a possible killer where she needed to live for the next two nights.

Chapter 8

The Suspicion

JENNY DID COME BACK OUT SHORTLY AFTER KATIE arrived at the desk.

"There you are. I was looking for you in the locker room."

"Huh," was all Katie could muster. "Zeke dropped me off, I got ready," she said, holding up her bathroom supplies, "and I came back out here. Not sure how we could have missed each other."

"Me neither, but I guess it doesn't matter. Are you all set? Need anything else?"

Wanting to get Jenny alone, she asked, "Want to take a stroll? I'd love to hear more about this place."

"Sure. Let me get my cardigan." Jenny walked off, but not as far as Katie expected her to. Apparently, there was a place where she hung her outerwear just around the corner. "All set."

"On the way, I'll drop my stuff off at the truck."

Jenny turned around as they reached the door and said, "Night, Zeke."

Katie listened carefully. Was that a romantic good night or a professional one?

Once outside, Katie asked, "Are you and Zeke an item? I mean, I'd understand if you were. He's very handsome."

Jenny blushed. "I wish we were an item, but he doesn't even see me. Last night I stayed late just to get a chance to talk with him alone, but Phil wouldn't leave the desk. Of course, that's when Rita and Karl showed up to talk about someone not picking up their towels after using the pool and wanted to know if Phil could look up the video footage from some specific time earlier that day. Do we really have a bunch of free time to go checking for pool towels?"

"I would think of all people, Phil would have plenty of time to do that. Sounds to me like Phil had a pretty cushy job. Midnight to eight? Sounds like at least six hours of alone time."

"If he were more reliable, maybe, but he struggles with getting here on time and staying awake."

Katie stopped walking, causing Jenny to stop as well. "That's something that doesn't make much sense to me. If Phil has a problem staying awake, why not swap him with Zeke. I've heard Zeke wants the late shift anyway. Wouldn't that make staying awake easier for Phil as well?"

Jenny blushed again, an even brighter shade of red this time. "We, the admin, have talked about swapping them, but I, well, I seem to come up with good reasons to keep Zeke on second shift."

"Any extraneous explanation for keeping him on second shift?" Katie gave Jenny a sly smile.

"I work nine to five, so I get to see Zeke at the end of my day. If he worked midnight to eight, I'd never see him accidentally. I know it's so selfish of me, and now with Phil gone, I'll probably lose Zeke anyway. This stinks."

"So, you never go out of your way to see Zeke any other time, just during your regular hours?"

"Not usually. Why?" Katie started walking in the direction of her truck again. Jenny joined.

"But you happened to stay last night. I don't remember you telling Officer Sullivan you saw Phil last night. From the sounds of it, you were probably one of the last people to see Phil alive."

"I'm sure I mentioned it to the second officer, but it didn't really seem to matter. I left before Zeke."

"Interesting."

Katie reached the truck and opened the back. "Want to see inside?"

"Sure."

Katie and Jenny clambered into the back of the truck. Jaspurr wasn't being held captive in the bed area and poked his sleepy face around the passenger seat to check out the new noises as Katie swapped out her shower caddy and towel for a small crossbody bag.

"Don't worry about us, Jaspurr."

"You have a cat in the truck." It was an observation, not a question. "Does he stay with you all the time?"

Katie looked quizzically at Jenny. "Where else would he stay?"

"Do you live in this truck full time?" She gazed around, taking in the space.

"Very soon it will be our only residence. I'm currently finishing up my lease for an apartment I can no longer afford. When that happens, we're on our own. I've got to make this business work."

"That's a lot of pressure to put on yourself. And this seems very small."

"My plan is to continue doing exactly what we did this weekend. Arrange for places to put up shop for a period of time and hopefully gain use of the local facilities, whatever that looks like. I've heard of people getting gym memberships for that purpose, so that'll be my next adventure. For now, I'm going to enjoy wherever life takes me."

"I could never take a risk like that. I like things to be predictable."

Jenny and Katie exited the truck. Once locked up, they walked along the same path Katie had taken Jaspurr earlier.

"Is that why you work a job where you make the schedule."

"Sure is. I know exactly what every day will look like. It's a great place to work, great benefits and the view isn't too bad either."

"The ocean or Zeke?"

Jenny smiled. "Both."

A measure of time passed in silence as they took in

the salty air and stretched their legs. "So, what do you think happened to Phil? You were here last night. Do you have a guess?"

"My guess is the same as it's always been. I think Phil got stuck in the freezer and no one heard him yelling for help."

"The freezer supposedly had a way to make sure you couldn't get locked in. If it was broken, that's one thing, but if the police find it was operational, you have a homicide on your hands."

"I guess that piece of information is going to be very important."

"Very," Katie reiterated. "Any chance you could put in a call to Leo to see if he would tell you? Has the walk-in freezer been cleared for use, or is it still an active crime scene?"

"That's a good question. I'm guessing the director would know that, but he's gone home for the weekend. Do you think I should call Leo to ask?"

Katie stopped, turned at a right angle to face Jenny and grabbed her shoulders. "To the police, this may simply look like an accident, a lazy employee who wasn't paying attention. To us, this is Phil. He's a co-worker. A person who matters. We should make sure we're helping the police in any way we can. It's our responsibility to get any details we can remember back to the police as well. It's practically our civic duty."

She was laying it on thick. Any other ice cream truck owner would keep their nose clean and drive off into the sunset on Sunday, but Katie felt a responsibility to Phil to make sure his—possible—killer was brought to justice and the motive was uncovered. Could it have been just an employee who wasn't willing to wait around for their turn at the shift differential, or was there something more sinister happening at The Pine Knoll Retirement Community?

"I'll do it. I'll call Leo. Let's go back so I can find his number."

"Actually, he gave me his card." Katie pulled the card out of her bag and handed it to Jenny.

"I do have my cell phone."

"Now's as good a time as any. What will you say?" Katie knew what she wanted Jenny to ask, but she couldn't be too pushy.

"A little small talk then ask if that emergency safety thing was in working order. How does that sound?"

"Sounds good to me. Might need a couple follow-up questions if it was fixed, like, was there anything else in the freezer that seemed out of place? Oh, and you can ask if it's still a crime scene."

"I'm sure the director knows."

"But the director isn't here to ask, and he won't know if you know or not. You can just pretend you need to..." Katie thought, but only for a moment. "You can ask if I'm all set to get my ice cream out tomorrow. He knows that's legit."

Katie and Jenny sat on the next bench. Jenny took out her phone and dialed the number for Officer Sullivan, putting it on speaker as she set it down between them.

"Officer Sullivan." He didn't say more than just his name.

"Hey, Leo. It's Jenny over at The Pine Knoll Retirement Community. I had Katie ask me if she could go in the walk-in to get the ice cream she stored in there, but I didn't know if it was still an active crime scene."

"As far as I know, we don't need anything else from you or your facility. Unless something surprising comes back from the medical examiner, it appears to have just been an accident."

Katie mouthed, 'Why?' but no sound came out.

"Why do you think it was an accident? Was there something we didn't see."

"From everything we gathered in the freezer, Phil was in there attempting to fix the emergency latch. There were a number of tools in there with him near the latch, but it was clearly still not working. There was also a brick just inside the door to the walk-in freezer we suspect he had propped it open with. The only trouble with that plan is when you go to test the latch after you think it's fixed. Everything points to this being a tragic accident."

"Thank you for the information. I'll let Katie know she can get her ice cream out of the freezer. If you do find you need anything else, don't hesitate to ask."

"Thank you, Jenny. I hope you can enjoy your weekend now."

"Good night."

Jenny tapped the screen, ending the call.

"I guess that's that. They're considering it an accident, and it seems like they have evidence to support it."

Katie considered her options. She could agree with Jenny in order to keep her in a positive mood, or Katie could pursue what she believed was intentional.

"Well, I guess we can head back and get that ice cream out of the freezer."

The pair of women stood and headed back in the direction of the retirement home.

"How is it you came to work here, anyway?" Katie asked.

"I got a degree in elementary education and physical education but couldn't find a job. When this one opened up, my mother saw it in the paper and suggested I apply. I never thought I'd get the job in a million years, but it's remarkable how similar it is to being a physical education teacher."

Katie laughed. "I didn't expect that answer. Well, do you plan to stay or are you still applying to elementary schools?"

"I'll stay as long as they'll have me. I enjoy working with this population more that I predicted. I took the job as a filler and really grew to love it."

"Everyone deserves to love their job. I'm in my mid-forties and still trying to figure out what I want to be when I grow up." Together they laughed and shared easy conversation on their way back.

"Just so I'm clear, who is working starting at midnight, in case I need to use the facilities?"

"Sadie will come on. She knows about you, so just press the bell, and she'll let you in."

"That will work perfectly. Thank you for working with me on all this." Katie stopped at her truck.

"Didn't you want to come in to get your ice cream?" Jenny asked.

"I was thinking about it, and I didn't sell enough to make room in the working freezers in the truck to add another. I'll get it tomorrow if I need it. Thanks for checking."

"I'm not usually here on Saturdays, but I will be here for your open hours. If you need me, call my cell."

"Will do. Have a nice evening."

Katie climbed into her truck with a plan.

"Hey, Jaspurr. Want to know what Mommy's going to do tonight?"

Chapter 9

The Details

KATIE PREPARED FOR BED. SHE BROUGHT DOWN THE ladder and turned back the covers. Being May in Maine, the weather was perfect for sleeping with the roof vent open. There was no precipitation in the forecast, and she was thankful for a pleasant first night sleeping in the ice cream truck.

"You know Jaspurr, we should name the truck. Let's start brainstorming ideas. Scoopmobile. Get the Scoop. Nah, that's more of a business name. I want a name we can use when we're talking about the truck." Jaspurr leapt up onto the bed with Katie and bumped the top of his head into her elbow. She lifted her arm for him to curl up with her. "Let's sleep on it. Maybe when we go meet Sadie in the morning, we'll have a better idea."

The day had been a whirlwind. Katie had driven to her first gig with the ice cream truck, discovered one freezer wasn't working properly, located a dead body and met several suspects. She expected the worst-case scenario to be a disappointed customer when she ran out of Death by Chocolate Chip, but this was far more interesting.

Having never been involved in an investigation, Katie thought she quite enjoyed the puzzle aspect. She'd gone to escape rooms before with colleagues at her various jobs and read countless murder mysteries, but this was completely new territory. While she laid in bed falling asleep, she wondered if maybe she could have been a detective if she'd made different choices earlier in life.

When her alarm went off at seven, she quickly hopped up and banged her head on the roof of the truck, waking Jaspurr in the process. "Darn you, Coco." She rubbed the tender spot on her forehead. "I guess my subconscious named her Coco last night." Jaspurr barked his approval, she hoped, and curled up in the cubby currently missing a towel.

Though Katie had showered last night, she fully intended on getting to Sadie's desk as early as possible to meet her and avoid as much traffic from residents as possible. The towel from last night was hanging on a hook next to the ladder she left down last night, and Katie grabbed it when she reached the floor. Thinking ahead, she had set out clothes for this morning knowing a walk with Jaspurr would need to be either a first or second priority. Since he was already back to sleep, she figured it could be second.

The walk to the front door was decidedly chillier this morning. A stunning fog had settled over the beach and hadn't burned off yet. Katie made a mental note to get up early tomorrow as well to see this beautiful sight again.

She pressed a button to the right of the front door, and a loud buzzer went off. Through the door, Katie could see a perky, college-age woman sitting at the desk, grinning from ear to ear. A new sound rang out, and the woman at the desk motioned for Katie to enter.

"Good morning, and welcome to Pine Knoll. You must be Katie."

"How did you know? Did Jenny relay my stunning beauty in such detail I couldn't be missed?"

"You're here just past seven in your pajamas. I can't think of anyone else buzzing in under those circumstances."

"Fair enough."

"Did you need to get to the locker room?"

"Well, I do, but I wanted to know how you like working here. I've gotten such a good vibe from everyone, I'm considering applying if the ice cream truck thing doesn't work out." She laughed and hoped it was convincing.

"We all love working here. It's a great environment, and the administration is caring and responsive."

"Don't be offended, but you seem pretty young to already be able to have that opinion."

"I'm going to school for communications, so this is just part time until I get to be administration myself. I'm always learning and trying to apply what I'm getting from my classes." Her smile was really a part of her personality and shown even brighter when she was talking about her passion.

"Pine Knoll would be smart to keep you. Are you working these weekend shifts so it doesn't conflict with your classes?"

"That's right. I figure if I can keep this job for four years, I'll have gained some great experience and be able to pay my bills."

Katie figured that eliminated her as a suspect for two reasons. She wasn't trying to go for Phil's position, nor was she in any kind of conflict with Phil because their schedules didn't cross. If she was right, Sadie might not even know what happened.

"So, did you hear about Phil?"

Her face fell. "Zeke told me. Heartbreaking."

"I'm sorry for your loss. Did you know him well?"

"I never really encountered Phil outside of emails and the occasional meeting organized by admin. Did you know him?"

"I sort of discovered him yesterday with Jenny."

"Oh, that's just awful. How are you doing?"

"I'll be fine. We were interviewed by the police, and it sounds like they think it was just a terrible accident. He was fixing the emergency latch that should have saved his life, but it wasn't working when he got trapped. That's what I'm gathering, anyway."

"From what I know about Phil, he's never fixed anything... in his life. I'm not trying to make a joke out of it, but he hardly shows up from what Zeke says. When he does, it's the bare minimum. He's employed from midnight to eight for a reason."

"What's that?"

"Almost no contact with other humans and zero responsibilities. Originally, they had a really hard time filling the position, and he's been here for a while. He keeps getting warnings, but they never let him go."

"So I've heard."

"Pretty bad when you've been here less than twenty-four hours and already know the dirt."

Katie smiled and leaned in. "Isn't that part of the fun of going to a new place?"

"I guess it can be."

"Well, before I use the bathroom, could you walk me back to the freezer. I want to know that my ice cream survived the investigation yesterday. No joke intended either."

Sadie stood. "No problem. I'll take you back there and then let you into the locker room." She walked around the corner of the desk and escorted Katie to the far end of the building as Jenny had done yesterday, just in her pajamas. When they got to the freezer, Sadie said, "Here we are." She pulled open the door. "I'll just hold this open while you're in there. Can't afford two accidents in two days, now, can we?"

"Absolutely not. My ice cream truck is scheduled to open at eleven. I'm guessing someone would come looking for me if I wasn't there to open it."

Katie explored the inside of the freezer, carrying her caddy and towel, looking for the emergency latch she never knew existed before. "Must be a newer thing. I worked my fair share of restaurant jobs over the years and never had of an emergency latch."

"Me neither, but I've never worked in food service. This is the first one I've seen and never been in." Sadie peered in from her position outside the open door. "I'm staying out here. Safer that way." Katie turned to see a reserved smile this time on Sadie's face.

"I'll take all the risks." Katie walked to the back where she had placed her tubs of ice cream only yesterday. "Still here and feels plenty frozen. Don't need them yet, but it's nice to know I have them."

Before leaving, she noticed there were no tools anywhere to be seen. Assuming the police had taken or moved them, she looked closer at the latch. There wasn't a mark or scratch to imply someone had been working on it. She searched all around, wondering if the broken part might be above, below or to the side, but found no evidence of any kind of work being done on the inside of the freezer door.

"And you say Phil doesn't fix anything?"

"Not to my knowledge. Never heard of him fixing anything, anyway. Even the email Jenny sent about Phil putting out your tables and chairs went unanswered. I'm pretty sure it wasn't Phil who did it."

That didn't make any sense to Katie. "Any idea when Jenny sent that email?"

"Not that I remember off the top of my head, but I could check when you're in the locker room if that helps."

Katie walked out, and Sadie shut the freezer door,

pushing it closed a second time for good measure. "Wouldn't want to lose all this food if the door's not shut tight."

They walked to the locker room where Sadie swiped her card to let Katie in. "I really appreciate you looking up that email about the tables and chairs. I know it's a silly little detail, but I'd hate if anything was missed and maybe an extra question or set of eyes could have been the answer."

"Not a problem at all. Take your time, and I'll see you when you're done. I'm not off until noon."

"Noon?" Katie questioned. "Why not eight?"

"I work the weekend shifts, remember. Two twelve-hour shifts."

"Gotcha." Katie was sure she knew that and had just forgotten. "Maybe you'll be able to get some ice cream at the end of your shift too."

"You can bet on it." Sadie allowed the door to close on the fitness center, and Katie carried her towel and caddy into the bathroom to freshen up. She had slept well, and the mattress was comfortable, but she needed to look into different pillows. As the steam escaped the room, she had a renewed drive to figure out what detail had been missed.

"Oh, hey, Katie." The bubbly college student was back at her desk ready to change the world. "I found that email. Want to see it?"

"Yes, please. Thank you." Katie went to the back side of the desk when Sadie waved for her to join on that side. She read the email, silently, asking Phil specifically to bring the tables and chairs from storage out to the front maple tree for the next day's event. "Looks like it was sent Thursday night at five. Jenny must have been wrapping up for the night."

"'Those tables and chairs would get ruined pretty quickly if they were left out all the time, Maine weather and all, so I'm sure she wanted them to go out at the last minute. Phil could have easily waited until seven in the morning. From what I understand, Randall's shift is pretty busy with everyone being awake and needing things all the time. I'm only busy from eight to noon, and not constantly, so I feel like I got the good shift."

"As long as everyone likes their shift, there's really no reason to complain, is there."

"Not really. Anything else I can do for you this fine morning?"

"I do have one more request." After Sadie assured her she would perform the requested task, Katie was ready to head out.

"If you want to meet my cat, Jaspurr, feel free to come out before eleven, but make sure to stop by for a scoop before you leave." She turned and made her way to the exit.

"A cat? I hope I have a break where I can meet him. See you later."

Katie waved goodbye before letting the doors close behind her. Once out of Sadie's view, she raced over to her truck and got ready in record time. Jaspurr was already holding his leash and harness when she stopped in front of him to give him some necessary chin scratches.

His adorable little face stretched out and accepted the gesture.

"Sorry I took so long. Let's go for our walk." Jaspurr stepped into his harness and Katie secured it. They made the same rounds as their first walk, with Katie accepting the extra pull on the leash when they approached the walkway down to the beach. "Don't want to go to the beach again?" she asked, and he gave her the feline version of side eye as he picked up the pace.

When they returned to the truck and Jaspurr was happily nibbling on his breakfast, a knock came on the driver's side window. Katie was surprised and pleased to see Officer Sullivan waiting for her.

Chapter 10

The Scoop

KATIE WAS OPENING HER SALES WINDOW AND SLIDING the awning into place two minutes before eleven. The residents, many of whom she recognized from Friday, were waiting outside the building at a distance. As the seconds ticked by, the scooters and walkers crept closer. One person sat at a table with their back to the truck, no ice cream in sight.

"If Jenny said you are allowed, I'm ready," Katie hollered out the opening in the side of the truck. While they made their way to her, she checked on Jaspurr one last time by stepping up onto the lowest rung of the ladder leading up to the bed. She knew he had snacks and water, but hoped he wouldn't try to escape just to prove his quirky orange-cat status.

By some miracle, the Mitchells made it to her first—probably because no one else wanted to be told off by Rita for cutting in line.

"Rita, you ready for that single scoop of Blueberry

Buckle on a sugar cone?" She appeared to be speechless. "Or do you need to try a sample?" Katie laid on the charm.

"I'll risk it," Rita whispered behind her hand for only Katie to hear.

"And you, Mr. Mitchell?" Katie started to scoop Rita's cone while she waited for Karl's answer.

"I'll go with Sugar on Snow again. Two scoops in a waffle cone this time. I'm feeling adventurous." He laughed from the belly. "You're too good to us, Katie. We hope you'll come back after this weekend."

She handed the single scoop to Rita. "Guess we'll see if I have time in my schedule and if Jenny wants be back."

"No question," Jenny responded from around the corner where Katie hadn't noticed her standing. "Told you I'd be here during your open hours."

"You sure did. Thanks for the support. Want to come scoop?"

Jenny trotted around the Mitchells and entered the truck from the back. "How about I take orders and money and you scoop. We'll be much faster that way."

"Sounds good." She leaned far over the counter and handed Karl his double scoop in a waffle cone. "Make sure I see you two tomorrow before I head out."

"We'll be back later tonight. Don't you worry." Rita held her cone in the air as she moved the walker with one hand and shuffled to a table, Karl hot on her heels.

The following ten or so orders were simple and provided good conversation, especially from people making suggestions about what she should do in the area on a Saturday night.

Sadie came out briefly about noon and handed Katie a paper. "Got everything you asked for with times. I hope it helps."

"Well, can I get you an ice cream before you leave for the day? On me." Katie smiled and slid the folded paper into her back pocket.

Sadie examined the chalkboard. "I think I'll go with Death by Chocolate Chip. Sounds perfect."

"Cone? Dish?"

"I'll go with a dish please, two scoops." Katie opened the freezer lid and started scooping.

"How was your night?" Jenny asked Sadie.

"Pretty boring until I got to meet Katie this morning."

"I think we've all grown to like Katie in the twenty-four hours we've known her," Jenny stated.

Katie handed the dish to Sadie. "Not quite twenty-four, but I'll take it."

"I'm going to sit and enjoy my ice cream." Sadie sat at the table with the unknown guest and said nothing to him.

More residents slowly trickled out of the building, some probably being responsible and waiting until after they had eaten lunch. The face Katie was pleased to see walking in her direction was Randall.

"Good morning, ladies. How are we doing on this fine Saturday."

Jenny responded first. "Doing great. Yourself?"

"I figured I'd come chat with Katie before going in to

relieve the afternoon desk attendant for her to come get an ice cream. Any update?"

Katie leaned in to keep her question for Randall between just the two of them. When she stood after asking, he said, "I'll go relieve her and get my ice cream when I return."

"Sounds good."

Randall did just that. He turned and walked to the front door, entering confidently. A woman who looked to be of a similar age to Katie came out to the truck and ordered a single scoop of Sweet Strawberries and Cream in a plain cone, thanked Katie and Jenny, and returned to her job. Unlike the rest of the staff, there was no small talk or pleasantries.

"Maybe consider her for the graveyard shift."

"Why's that?" Jenny asked.

"Because she has the personality of a cemetery groundskeeper."

"That's cruel." However, Jenny laughed. "But accurate."

When she entered the building, Randall returned to the ice cream truck.

Jenny stepped up to help. "What can we get you?"

"I'll take a single scoop of raspberry sorbet, please. Haven't tried anything like that in a while."

Katie scooped then walked to the back of the truck, opening the door and hopping down. Randall met her at the back corner.

"Did you find anything on the video footage of the

outside of the building Thursday night into Friday morning?"

"It's a total mystery. There is no footage from the outside cameras. I checked the inside ones again, the ones I checked before, and those are fine, but it's like someone deleted the exterior ones."

Katie pulled a folded piece of paper from her back pocket. "What's really odd is that earlier this morning, the outside camera recordings were just fine. In fact, another employee was able to pull them up and give me the people who were coming and going along with the times." She looked Randall in the eye. "Looks like you were here and didn't mention it."

"Well, I might have stopped by to grab something I forgot. Happens all the time."

"You forgot you stopped by on the night someone died?"

"I guess so."

"Any idea how the exterior camera recordings are gone now but they were fine earlier this morning?"

"Maybe I made a mistake. I can go take another look."

At this point, the man sitting with his back to the ice cream truck stood and turned around.

"Nice to see you this morning, Officer Sullivan," Katie announced. "I wanted to introduce you to a member of the staff here who you might not have met yet. Mr. Randall Quagmire is the daytime desk attendant. He happened to be here the night Mr. Rainey died in the freezer. Did you by any chance, Officer Sullivan, find any fingerprints on those tools in the freezer?"

"Funny you should ask. We did have them examined this morning—on a hunch—and found no prints matching Mr. Rainey. Looks like our assumption about Phil working on the freezer emergency latch was incorrect."

"I wonder how they got into the freezer without him touching them."

Randall bolted, attempting to take off down the trail Katie had walked with Jaspurr this weekend. Luckily, when Katie contacted Officer Sullivan earlier this morning—on a hunch—he was proactive enough to bring a few of his co-workers with him, also in plain clothes. At the very first bench along the trail, Frankie, who Katie had met previously, elbowed Randall in the gut, dropping him to the path in a matter of seconds.

Officer Sullivan ran up, Katie close behind. "Randall Quagmire, you're under arrest for the murder of Philip Rainey. You have the right to..." Once Officer Sullivan was done reading Randall his Miranda rights, Katie had a few questions for him.

"I know you don't have to answer any of my questions, and the wonderful police officer here is going to advise you against saying anything, but why? Why kill Phil? I get that it's probably annoying that he doesn't do his fair share, but it just doesn't make any sense."

"How did you know?" He was either ignoring her question or couldn't process what she was asking as he was lifted from the ground, cuffs around his wrists.

"First, you told me Phil froze to death. No one had said anything about the cause of death, but you jumped to one. Second, you lied about what you saw on the security camera footage. Rita and Karl had no reason to lie. Once I caught you in one lie, I asked Sadie to do some digging in the cameras. I had every reason to believe you actually did forget the footage on the exterior cameras and would come back to delete it if I didn't get to her first. Looks like I was right."

Officers Leo Sullivan and Frankie June escorted Randall back to the parking lot where they stopped near Katie's truck. The residents, who had all stopped eating to gawk, watched everything unfolding.

"So," Katie asked again, "why?"

"Phil was lazy. He was a security risk, and him working here put all of these good people in danger."

"Are you saying having you work her made them safer?"

"I know it sounds backward, but I wanted to get Zeke into the position he wanted and hire someone new who could be a better team player."

"So, you staged it to look like Phil was working on the freezer. He went in, probably to get something for you, and you kicked the brick out of place, leaving him in there all night. Sound accurate?"

Short of nodding, Randall looked at her with sad eyes. "I hope whoever takes my place loves this job and these residents as much as I did." He then proceeded to start walking toward a waiting police car Katie hadn't noticed earlier, two officers holding tightly to his arms.

* * *

At the end of her final shift on Sunday, Katie packed up to go back to her apartment for the last time. She returned to the building, greeted by the cemetery groundskeeper, and retrieved her two extra tubs of ice cream, never having needed them.

"Can you believe how it took such an odd turn of events for this murder to be solved?" she said to Jenny as she used her card to gain access to the staff areas.

"If your truck freezer had been working properly, you'd never have come back here with me. If you hadn't come back, I guarantee this would have been deemed an accidental death with no one looking into it enough to find Randall's lies. If he had thought to delete the exterior footage on his own, there would be no reason to suspect him."

"It really is a good thing I asked Sadie to make copies before she came out for ice cream."

Together, they began to enter the walk-in freezer to get the remaining two tubs of ice cream, but Jenny decided against it, holding the door for Katie. Stepping in and carefully avoiding the location that had previously been occupied by Phil's body, Katie picked up the first tub and brought it out to Jenny.

"Where will you go next?" she asked as she accepted the heavy cylinder.

"I don't have a plan yet. I put out some feelers for similar gigs to this one but haven't heard back. If I need to, I'll contact some cities about food truck permits for street parking or farmers' markets. I'm also willing to do birthdays and weddings, so that will give me more options."

Katie returned to the back of the freezer to grab the second tub. When she exited, Jenny let the door close. "I'd be happy to give you a reference, for ice cream or future detective work. You were amazing."

"Thanks. I'm not sure where that came from, but it sure was interesting and a little fun. Didn't know I had that in me."

The two walked all the way back to the ice cream truck and packed away the two tubs in spaces that had been made when she ran out of Banana Blitz and Luscious Licorice.

"I'd love to come back again, if you found the residents enjoyed the event enough to make it worth your while to host my return."

"I'm sure they will all want you back, but only if you can solve another murder as entertainment. I'll be hearing about and reliving this for months." She exaggerated the word months.

"I don't want anyone else to be in danger, but getting to solve another mystery would be the cherry on top."

"Your two biggest fans wanted me to say bye for them."

"The Mitchells?" Katie clarified. "Tell them, I'll be back."

Katie hopped up into the drivers' seat of her pink ice cream truck, affectionately named Coco, and gave Jaspurr a quick head rub. Closing the door on an adventurous weekend, Katie said, "I wonder what will happen on our next gig, Jaspurr?"

He barked and stretched out enough from his place on the passenger seat to head bump her elbow.

"Okay, okay. Let's get going home."

She put the truck in first gear and slowly pulled out of the parking lot, leaving behind several new friends and taking with her memories she'd never forget.

PLEASE LEAVE A REVIEW!

★★★★★

Virginia K Bennett

An Appetite for Solving Crime

THANK YOU FOR READING MY BOOK!

I WOULD LOVE TO READ YOUR FEEDBACK ON FACEBOOK, INSTAGRAM, AMAZON, OR SIMPLY SEND AN EMAIL TO:

authorvirginiakbennett@gmail.com

Also by Virginia K. Bennett

A Newfound Lake Cozy Mystery:

* * *

The Mysteries of Cozy Cove:

About the Author

When she's not writing on her couch with her two cats, Twyla and Geo, Virginia is busy teaching middle school math, grocery shopping, cooking or spending time with her husband and son. Together, her small family loves to go geocaching and visit theme parks.

Mysteries have always been an interesting challenge for Virginia, much like watching a magician perform. Unless you want to hear the entire thought process behind who she thinks is the killer and why, you might want to avoid watching any movies together.

The path to publishing a book is different for everyone and her path is full of twists and turns. Thank you to those who support the journey.

facebook.com/VirginiaKBennett

instagram.com/authorvkbennett

Made in the USA
Middletown, DE
25 July 2024

57987833R00060